Just Grace
Goes Green

Just Grace
Goes Green

BIG
PLAN

Written and illustrated
by
Charise Mericle Harper

sandpiper

Houghton Mifflin Harcourt
Boston New York

The text of this book is set in Dante.
The illustrations are pen and ink drawings digitally colored in Photoshop.

Library of Congress Cataloging-in-Publication Data is on file.

ISBN: 978-0-547-24821-9 pb

Printed in the United States of America

DOC 10 9 8 7 6 5 4

4500404373

For my editor, Margaret Raymo,
who is patient, kind, and creatively cool!

JUST GRACE GOES GREEN IS PRINTED
ON 100% RECYCLED PAPER

This means it . . .

1 contains 100% post-consumer fiber
2 is certified EcoLogo and processed
   chlorine-free
3 is certified FSC recycled
4 is manufactured using biogas energy

Using recycled paper instead of regular
paper in *Just Grace Goes Green* helps the
environment in the following ways:

1 Saves the equivalent of 17 mature trees
2 Reduces solid wastes by 1,081 pounds
3 Reduces the quantity of water used by
   10,196 gallons
4 Reduces air emissions by 2,098 pounds
5 Reduces natural gas consumption by
   2,478 cubic feet by using biogas

THINGS YOU CAN CHANGE

1 Your underpants. Hopefully every day, and if you are a girl probably without your mother having to remind you about it one hundred and one times.

GIRLS' UNDERPANTS   **BOYS' UNDERPANTS**

2 Your friends. Sometimes you might think that you have the perfect number of friends, but then you add a new friend to the list and suddenly you can't believe that it used to be different, because now it seems so just right perfect, and just maybe even better than before.

3 Your mind. So that if you at first thought one thing, but then some time goes by and now you think another thing, then that's okay.

THINGS YOU CANNOT CHANGE

1 Your family. Even if sometimes they absolutely and completely drive you crazy, and you can't even believe you are really related to them.

2 Your messy room. No matter how much you clean it up, the new stuff you bring into it always makes it messy again. Though some rooms are more messy than others. Compared to Mimi's room, my room is the castle of clean!

3 Your name on a teacher's list, even if it is marked in pencil. I know this because I used to be called Grace, but now I'm called Just Grace, and it will probably be that way in my school life forever and ever. Plus, my name is now not even next to the other Graces'!

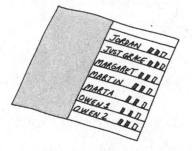

JORDAN
JUST GRACE
MARGARET
MARTIN
MARTA
OWEN 1
OWEN 2

MY NAME IN MISS LOIS'S BOOK

MISS LOIS VS. ME

Miss Lois is my teacher at school. If her wants and my wants were in a wrestling match, her wants would always win. That's how it goes with teachers and students. And that's why my wants are sitting in the corner feeling sad. It's no fun to always be the loser.

MY WANTS   **MISS LOIS'S WANTS**

Even though my wants are the always-losers, I don't hate Miss Lois.

THE NEW MISS LOIS

Miss Lois has been a more fun teacher lately. She used to be boring and serious most of the time, but now she is only those things some of the time. It's a big improvement! I think it's because she saw how much all her students loved Mr. Frank. He was fun 100 percent of the time. Mr. Frank was our student teacher, but he couldn't stay with us forever because he had to go back to school to finish off getting his teacher license. It's like a driver's license, except

when you get it you don't get to do something fun like drive a car—you just get to stand in front of a classroom and talk.

Since Mr. Frank left, Miss Lois has been

trying a lot of new things, and mostly that has been exciting for us. She likes to give out her new ideas on Monday mornings—that way she says we will be excited for the whole rest of the week about a fun, stimulating learning experience.

Stimulating means that the parts of your brain you use to learn stuff are excited and exploding like mini fireworks. Owen 1 said that Sunni's head was probably going to explode one day, because she is the smartest kid in our class and she really likes learning. Then he started asking her lots of questions so she would use her brain and make it blow up right then and there.

Sunni just turned around and called him a peon. Of course, Owen 1 didn't know what a peon was—none of us did. She is smart like that, and uses lots of words no one has ever heard of before. But for sure it was not a compliment, and since Owen 1 was being mean and is not one bit smart, I bet it meant something perfectly awful. I was definitely going to look it up in the dictionary. Mostly I don't like looking stuff up, but it's always good to know about new name-calling words, even if you're not supposed to be using them. Just in case.

WORD FOR LATER

WHAT MISS LOIS SAID

"Owen 1, if I have to tell you to stop talking one more time, I'm sending you down to the principal's office! Do you understand?" Owen 1 nodded his head yes, and Sunni smiled, and her perfectly round head did not explode.

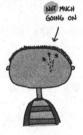

FIREWORKS INSIDE SUNNI'S HEAD

FIREWORKS INSIDE OWEN 1'S HEAD

WHAT MISS LOIS SAID NEXT

"Class, it's time for us to go green. Does anyone know what that means?" Everyone had lots of different answers.

WHAT GOING GREEN DOES NOT MEAN

 1   Studying frogs.

 2   Dressing up as Irish leprechauns.

 3   Getting free money.

 4   Eating lots of spinach or salad.

WHAT GOING GREEN DOES MEAN

Learning about new ways to save energy, recycle, and save the planet and its inhabitants, which means all the plants and animals and us. Miss Lois said our planet needed our help and we were all going to be superheroes of conservation and save the earth! Then she did something that was totally like Mr. Frank and not at all like Miss

9

Lois. She asked us to each design our own superhero costume.

When a project is fun, people sometimes want to do even more work than they are supposed to. This doesn't happen very often, so Miss Lois smiled when she said it was okay to design two different costumes if we wanted.

MY SUPERHEROES OF CONSERVATION

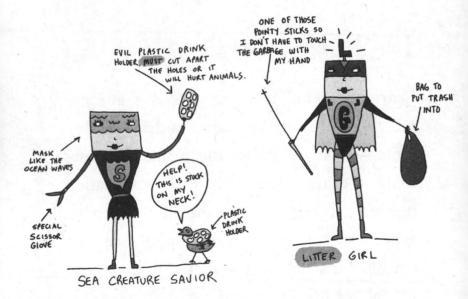

It was hard to get everybody to stop doing the fun part of saving the earth and concentrate on the learning part of saving the earth. Jane Dublin was especially unhappy when she found out that Miss Lois was not going to take our designs home and make us all real costumes to wear. Her costume was a pretty cool butterfly kind of thing. She would have sure looked great in it because she's got long, skinny legs kind of like a bug.

Other people, like Owen 1, didn't really do a very good job of thinking about their design as a real costume. It would have been really hard for him to even fit in his.

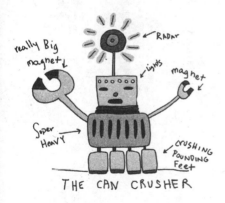

really Big magnet

RADAR

lights

magnet

Super Heavy

CRUSHING POUNDING Feet

THE CAN CRUSHER

OWEN 1'S COSTUME

Miss Lois tried to make everybody feel better by saying that all our designs would make great Halloween costumes. She just doesn't know that most boys would never wear superhero costumes when they could wear gross masks and creepy clothes dripping with fake blood instead.

EXTRA
EYE

BLOOD
DRIPPING
OFF HIM

SOMETHING
GROSS

SOME KIND
OF WEAPON

SUPERHERO   **SCARY GUY**

THREE WAYS TO SAVE THE EARTH

1. RECYCLE

This means you put things in special bins so that they can be used again to make new stuff, instead of just throwing them in the garbage.

THINGS YOU CAN RECYCLE

Paper Products

Plastic

 ← MOSTLY YOU CAN ONLY RECYCLE PLASTIC THAT HAS THIS SIGN AND THE NUMBER ONE OR TWO IN THE MIDDLE.

Glass

Foil

Cans

2. CONSERVE

This means if you are not going to be in a room, then you should turn out the light so you don't use up energy that you don't really need.

There are lots of way to conserve energy that were too hard for us to do. Things like making sure you have good windows in your house and lots of insulation in the walls. Insulation is padding stuff that is stuck in the walls of houses. Miss Lois said it was like the fluffy stuff inside winter jackets only it was for the house. She said it worked the same, and that is how people kept their houses warm and cozy in the wintertime.

Then she told us she did not want anyone to go home and knock holes in their walls to try to get a look and see if it was in there. As soon as she said this, Owen 1 said,

"Aww, man!" So you could tell that he was totally thinking of doing this exact thing.

Miss Lois said that conservation was some-thing we could all prac-

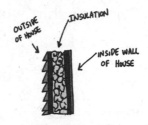

INSULATION IN A HOUSE WALL

tice at home right away. Marta said that she was going to try to get her little sister to stop playing with the toilet and flushing it all the time. Miss Lois said that was an excellent idea since every time you flush the toilet you use up around 3.5 gallons of water.

Sammy said he could just wear the same clothes every day—that way his mom wouldn't have to do any laundry and that would save water too. Miss Lois said that was an interest-ing idea but not necessary because being clean was important too. I think she was probably being like me and imagining what

Sammy's shirt would look like without being cleaned for an entire week.

SAMMY'S SHIRT

Miss Lois said conservation is important because it helps save the animals of the world and their natural habitats. Which means the places where they live in the wild . . . not so much the zoo, because zoo animals pretty much don't have to worry about their homes being taken away to build a road or a grocery store.

ZOO ANIMAL TALKING

3. REUSE

This means that instead of throwing something away you find someone who wants it and can use it, and then you sell it or give it to them. Miss Lois said lots of people donate clothes, computers, books, and even cars to people who need them.

WHAT I WAS THINKING NEXT

Sometimes if someone is giving me too much information, even if it is interesting and really important information like how to save the world, all I can think about is . . . *When is the talking going to stop so we can go do something else?*

Miss Lois didn't hear my secret thoughts because she just kept talking, and talking, and talking, right up until the bell rang for our break. "I'm passionate about being green," said Miss Lois, and then she finally let us go.

WHAT IS PASSIONATE

Passionate means that Miss Lois probably wishes she could spend her entire life working on saving the planet. And maybe I was right about that, because right after our break she said we were going to skip math and talk some more about being green.

LESS TALK, PLEASE

Miss Lois said it was time to stop talking and time to start doing. She said nobody could save the earth all alone. We all had to work together. She said it was time to team up. Miss Lois was acting like Mr. Frank again, because she even let us pick our own partners. Of course Mimi and I picked each other. I didn't get to work with her on the last school project because I was away in Chicago. After everyone picked a partner, Miss Lois gave us our green jobs.

JOB NUMBER ONE

Keep a chart about the way we are conserving energy and being green at home. Write down at least one conservation thing that we are doing every day. Keep the chart for two weeks.

JOB NUMBER TWO

Come up with a green project that we are passionate about and then put that plan into action. Miss Lois said it was important to not think too big. She said, "The best green plans are right in your very own backyard."

This was a little confusing, because Sandra Orr thought Miss Lois said that the best green *plants* were right in our very own backyard. So she put her hand up and said, "You're right! And I probably have the biggest green plant ever, because I am growing my very own pumpkin for Halloween, and those kind of plants take up the entire backyard. My dad is not happy about it, so Mom says this is the only year we are going to get to do it. Maybe the class can come over and see it, because it's really awesome!"

Max and Sammy both said they totally wanted to see it, and pretty soon everyone was excited about pumpkins and Halloween.

Miss Lois seemed a little confused and a little annoyed both at the same time. She wanted us all to be excited about saving water, saving paper, and saving metal cans, and not be talking about giant pumpkins instead.

THE NEW AND IMPROVED MISS LOIS

The old Miss Lois would have definitely been mad at us for not paying attention to her ideas, but the new Miss Lois said, "Okay, class, it's time for everyone to pick an animal mascot."

PUMPKIN VERSUS ANIMAL

WHO IS THE WINNER?

ANIMAL MASCOTS

Miss Lois said each group had to pick an animal from the endangered animals list as its mascot. Endangered animals are creatures that will go extinct if people do not stop destroying the natural places where they live. Stuff like cutting down trees or building houses and factories near their homes means that the animals have nowhere to go and no proper food to eat so they die. It's very sad.

Miss Lois said that it was important to know about all these endangered animals. And to know them better we each had to write a paragraph about our mascot animal and present it to the class.

Saving the planet was sounding a lot like regular schoolwork. I bet real superheroes don't have to write reports and do all sorts of projects. No wonder the earth was in trouble: nothing was probably ever getting done.

Sandra Orr put her hand up and said that protecting animals was really important, and that it was really sad that humans had ruined the earth because now there were no more unicorns left and it was too late to save them. Miss Lois said, "Yes, Sandra, saving animals is very important." She knew you couldn't say one thing about unicorns not being real animals or else Sandra would burst into tears and have to go home. That had happened before.

THE LIST

Even though the list of animals on the endangered list was super long, Mimi and I had no trouble picking out our favorite three animals. It was a little harder trying to decide which of the three would be best.

THE THREE TOP ANIMALS ON OUR LIST

RED PANDA

NUMBAT

SANDCAT

Finally we decided to pick the red panda because it was just so sad that an animal that cute could maybe go extinct, and then no one would ever see it again.

WHAT BOYS DO

All the boy groups picked weird and ugly animals for their mascots, stuff like rats, mice, and snakes. Max and Sammy said they picked the aye-aye because they liked saying the name a lot. The aye-aye was also a very weird-looking animal, so for sure they were probably excited about that too!

AYE-AYE

FINALLY

This was a school day that seemed like it was going to last forever, even with Miss Lois trying to be fun and full of new ideas like Mr. Frank.

I was so happy when it was all over and we could finally stop thinking about saving the earth and go home.

MIMI'S NEWS

The minute Mimi told me I said, "I can't believe you didn't tell me this before!" Not because it was a bad thing, but because it was a good thing, and how can you not tell your best friend a good thing the moment you find out about it? Mimi said that at first it sounded like a good thing but really when you thought about it, it was not a completely great thing after all, which is why she didn't tell me about it right away. She wanted it to sit in her brain so she could think about it a little bit first.

Mimi's brain is like that. It probably has all sorts of interesting things in there waiting to come out one day. My brain is 100 percent the opposite. It likes to let everything right out through my mouth the minute it knows about it.

THE THING

Mimi's cousin Gwen is coming to stay with Mimi for ten days. At first I thought this was a good thing because I love Gwen and we all have so much fun when she visits. But when Mimi told me the three bad things about it, it didn't seem so great anymore, at least not for Gwen.

1 Gwen was going to miss school, which is always a good thing, except she was going to have to hang out with Mimi's mom every day because Mimi was going to be at school. Plus, on top of that she was going to have to do all her homework anyway. How much fun was that going to be?

2 She was going to miss her birthday with her friends.

3 She was going to miss her mom and dad.

WHY GWEN HAS TO STAY WITH MIMI

Gwen's parents have to go to China for a big business meeting, and then after the meeting they are going on a mini vacation there, without Gwen. Mimi said, "At least they are not going somewhere really fun." But still they are going to be gone on her real birthday, which is completely not fair. Mimi said that Gwen is being brave and saying that she doesn't care about that part because when her parents get back she gets to have a super-big birthday party to make up for it. But I bet she is just acting about that, because if Mom and Dad missed my birthday I would for sure be sad.

Gwen's parents have a company that sells doorknobs and coat hooks and stuff like that. Last year Gwen gave me some fancy glass hooks for my room. They are nice, but not really the best invention ever, because as soon as you use them you can't see how great the hooks look anymore. I didn't say that, though, because that's not polite and I knew it was much better to just say thank you.

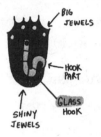

BEAUTIFUL HOOK　　　　**NOW YOU CAN'T SEE IT**

WHAT SAMMY SAID

When Sammy heard what Mimi and I were talking about he said, "I bet Gwen's parents work for a secret spy network and that's why they have to go to China." He said spies were always going to other countries to do their spy work. Usually they weren't allowed to bring their kids on missions, so that was probably why Gwen had to stay with Mimi's parents. Sammy thinks everyone is a spy. He even thought that Mrs. Witkins was a spy when I saw her climbing in and out of her basement window. Of course he was totally wrong.

Mimi rolled her eyes and said she was pretty sure that her aunt JoJo was not a spy. Sammy couldn't ask her any more about it because Max came up to him and said they had to go. Max and Sammy are taking Tae Kwon Do lessons. Max said he and Sammy can chop wood in half with their bare hands but they aren't allowed to do it outside of the Tae Kwon Do studio. This made Mimi roll her eyes again. Max and Sammy are definitely not as tough as they think they are, but we didn't say that because it was much easier to just say "Un-huh."

HOW TO MAKE SOMEONE FEEL WELCOME

1 Make a big sign and put it on the front lawn. If your friend's mom won't let you put it on the front lawn, then hang it up on a door.

2 Make sure the guest has some space to put her clothes, so empty out a few drawers and throw your friend's stuff in the closet.

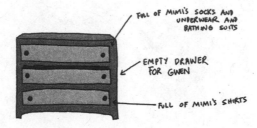

FULL OF MIMI'S SOCKS AND UNDERWEAR AND BATHING SUITS

EMPTY DRAWER FOR GWEN

FULL OF MIMI'S SHIRTS

3 Make signs so that the guest knows where things are.

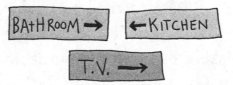

BATHROOM ➡   ⬅KITCHEN

T.V. ➡

4 Make the guest's bed nice and comfy, with pillows and stuffed animals that are cozy just in case she might have to cry.

HEART-SHAPED PILLOW

5 Buy her favorite snacks, even if they are the kind of snacks your friend's mom doesn't normally let her eat because they are not healthy and nutritious.

6 Be cheerful and don't fight with the guest, even if she is wrong and you are right.

SMILE IS ONLY ON THE OUTSIDE.

Mimi and I did the first four things to get ready for Gwen. The number five thing Mimi said she was going to ask her mom about. The number six thing we were saving until she got there, and I was hoping that we were never going to need it. But it was smart of Mimi to put it on the list, just in case.

SAVING THE WORLD AT HOME

Of course Miss Lois gave us homework, so before I even got to do my one conservation thing and put it on the chart, I had to read a whole lot of pages about recycling. At first I was really grumpy about it, but in the end it was pretty interesting and probably important. Mom and Dad already do lots of recycling stuff, so it wasn't so easy to think of something new that I could do by myself.

CONSERVATION THINGS THAT I DID NOT WANT TO DO

1 Turn off the TV and read a book instead. Read the book with a flashlight to save the energy of lighting up the whole room. I could have said use a candle, but Mom would never in a thousand years let me use a candle all by myself, especially if I was holding paper at the same time.

2 Wash my dishes by hand instead of putting them in the dishwasher.

3 Save my half-eaten baked potato from dinner so I could have it for lunch tomorrow. We really need a dog so that I don't feel so guilty about throwing food away. Even though it wasn't in Miss Lois's notes, I'm pretty sure throwing away food is bad for the earth.

**EARTH COMPLAINING
ABOUT WASTED FOOD**

MY ONE CONSERVATION THING

Finally I just decided to walk around the house and turn off all the lights in the rooms that no one was using. At least it was something. I didn't know Mom was in the basement until she screamed in the dark. She was okay, though, and hardly got mad, even though she bumped her head on the low pipe in the laundry room.

Turned off all lights in the house that were not being used by Mom, Dad, or me.

HOW TO SAY GOOD NIGHT TO YOUR BEST FRIEND

Mimi and I have our bedrooms right across from each other, so we are especially lucky best friends. Most nights we flash our lights at each other to say good night. Tonight when I looked out my window, Mimi was pointing to her stuffed squirrel, Willoughby. We have a secret stuffed animal code so we can tell each other how happy or not happy we are. We used to do flashlight Morse code to tell each other stuff, but it was too confusing and not fun so we stopped.

MIMI'S CODE

HAPPY	**NOT SO HAPPY**	**UNHAPPY**

HE HAS A VERY SOFT TAIL.

MIMI'S AUNT MADE THIS FOR HER

MIMI HATES THIS BUNNY. SHE SAYS IT'S CREEPY.

Willoughby **Pig Pig** **Bunny**

MY CODE

HAPPY	NOT SO HAPPY	UNHAPPY

I MADE CHIP-UP WITH MIMI. I ♥ LOVE HIM.

PUMPKIN DOLL GRANDMA BOUGHT ME BECAUSE SHE SAID IT HAD HAIR LIKE MINE.

BONNY I NEVER REALLY LIKED.

Chip-Up	Rachel	Fluffy

Mimi was probably happy because Gwen was coming the next day for her visit. Our moms weren't going to let us stay home from school so we could meet her— that's why we had to make all the signs for her. That way even though we weren't there, she would still know that we were thinking about her and were happy that she was visiting. I don't know why, but it was way more fun to be thinking about Gwen and saving her than it was to be thinking about saving the earth.

WHAT I LEARNED AT SCHOOL THAT I DIDN'T KNOW BEFORE

Miss Lois said that if all the garbage regular people throw away in our country of America was a big disgusting pie, this was how it would look.

GARBAGE PIE

She said only a little bit of this pie gets recycled or reused—most of it just gets thrown away. Miss Lois said there are two ways to get rid of garbage once it has been collected by the garbage men.

1 Burn it in an incinerator—a big furnace made specially to burn garbage.

2 Bury it in a landfill—a big hole in the ground where you dump garbage.

She said both of these are not great solutions to the garbage problem, but it was all there was.

Robert Walters said, "What's wrong with burning stuff up? That sounds like a fun job. Wow! I bet you get to use one of those fire guns like the kind the guys use on TV to kill aliens. That would be so awesome!" Miss Lois said she did not know anything about killing aliens on TV, but she was 100 percent sure that the people who worked at the incinerators did not use fire guns or any kind of weapons.

COMIC STRAIGHT FROM THE BRAIN
OF ROBERT WALTERS

Even though I know I'm not supposed to doodle or draw comics in class, I couldn't help myself. I just have to be more sneaky and not get caught, is all. With Miss Lois being all passionate about the earth, it was a little bit easier because she was not watching us as closely as usual. Miss Lois had a lot more stuff to say about incinerators and landfills, which was good because it gave me time to finish my drawing.

I'm lucky that I can draw and listen at

the same time. That way even if I got surprise-tested with questions I would still know the answers, and Miss Lois would have to be impressed. Miss Lois would suddenly know how amazing I was at paying attention and she would feel bad that she had been thinking not-paying-attention thoughts about me.

When this happens to someone it's called eating crow. You don't actually have to eat a crow. It's just a saying that means you have to say sorry for what you did or said, and probably sometimes doing that kind of thing might be as hard, or as gross, as eating a real crow.

We just finished reading a play in class last week, so now I know all about how they work. If I were in a play with Miss Lois right now, this is how it would go.

MISS LOIS EATS CROW

A PLAY

(The scene takes place in a classroom just like ours, but the desks are fancy and new and definitely don't have gross stuff stuck on the bottom of them.)

(Miss Lois looks mean and grumpy.)

GRRR.

MISS LOIS: Just Grace, are you not paying attention again? Can you tell me why incinerators are still not the best way to dispose of garbage?

(I look up at her happy and smiling, not at all scared, because I know the answer.)

ME: Well, Miss Lois, when you burn up garbage, the smoke from the fire is full of pollution, and that is bad for the earth. Plus, when everything is all burned up, you still have to bury all the black gross ashes from the fire and that is bad too.

(Miss Lois looks a little surprised.)

MISS LOIS: Just Grace, I don't suppose you know what is wrong with burying garbage in a landfill?

(I smile sweetly, not sneakily.)

ME: Actually, Miss Lois, I do. Just because garbage is buried and we can't see it that doesn't mean it disappears. The garbage under the earth just sits there for hundreds of years, and sometimes all the bad poisons from the rotting garbage go into the earth and then get into the rivers and the lakes. This is bad for people and animals and it can make us all sick.

(Miss Lois is shocked. She has her hands over her mouth. She cannot believe that the 100 percent perfect answers have come out of my mouth.)

MISS LOIS: Just Grace! I can't believe I ever doubted you! I'm so sorry! You have been paying the most perfect attention ever! I think it's time to change someone's name in the attendance notebook.

And then she would erase the *Just* part of my name in the notebook and we would smile all happy-like at each other.

THE END

HOW TO NOT GET CAUGHT

Miss Lois asked Valerie Newcome, who was sitting right in front of me, a question about plastics and then I knew I had forgotten to be paying attention the whole time I was thinking about Miss Lois eating crow. I didn't even know we were talking about plastic. I thought we were still talking about garbage.

Sometimes when you shrink low in your seat Miss Lois will know that you are trying to disappear, so she will pick you out on purpose, because kids who are trying to disappear probably have not been paying attention and don't know the answer. It's really hard to sit up straight and pretend you know what is going on when that is not what is true, but you have to do it because that is the only way to save yourself. It's kind of like what people are supposed to do when they meet a bear.

Your body doesn't want to do it, so your brain has to take over and force it even though it is scary and it doesn't feel right.

HOW TO SAVE YOUR LIFE FACING A BEAR

LIE ON THE GROUND AND PLAY DEAD. DON'T MOVE.

HOW TO SAVE YOUR LIFE FACING MISS LOIS

DO NOT LOOK SCARED. LOOK STRAIGHT AHEAD.

Valerie Newcome did not know the answer, and I could tell that right away because she was slouching even more. Miss Lois said that if Valerie had been paying attention she would know that Americans use over two million plastic bottles every hour and that most of those were thrown away and not recycled. This was unbelievable, but not as unbelievable as what happened next.

Valerie put her hand up and said, "I'm sorry, Miss Lois. I'm having trouble paying attention because I'm just so excited about my superheroes of conservation project. I already started on it and I can't wait to show everybody. Can I show everyone now what I've done?" Miss Lois looked surprised too. Valerie is not always the best worker, and she does a lot of not paying attention.

What Valerie showed us was for sure not what Miss Lois was expecting, because she looked even more surprised than before.

Valerie held up two of her Barbie dolls dressed as superheroes. She showed us the picture she had drawn too, so everyone could see what a good job she had done making the actual real-life costumes.

VALERIE'S SUPERHEROES

STAR HEADBAND SO THAT WE DO NOT FORGET ABOUT THE UNIVERSE

CAPE WITH RECYCLING TRIANGLES ON IT

REAL GLOBE

TWIST TIE

PULL TAB FROM CAN

PLASTIC MILK BOTTLE TOP

BOTTLE CAP FROM GLASS BOTTLE

PIECES OF PAPER

SHE HELPS TO REMIND PEOPLE TO RECYCLE.

ENVIRO-GAL   **GOTTA-GO-GREEN-GIRL (GGGG)**

Miss Lois said that all the boys had to stop laughing immediately. I think boys sometimes laugh because they are embarrassed about liking girl stuff. Even though

I'm too old to like Barbie dolls anymore, I thought Valerie's superheroes were pretty good. Miss Lois put them on the table at the front of the class so that everyone could have a closer look at lunchtime. And that was how I didn't get caught not paying attention.

LUNCHTIME

Mimi was so impressed by Enviro-Gal and Gotta-Go-Green-Girl that she said we had to make real superheroes too. She said we could make a whole scene out of clay and craft stuff, and it could show our superheroes coming to help save the red panda, which is perfect because that is our endangered animal mascot. Mimi loves clay or any kind of supplies to make stuff that stands up on its own. She doesn't like drawing very much but she makes really fun, cool model projects all the time.

WHAT MIMI MADE FOR ME LAST WEEK

At lunchtime Mimi told me about all the things I had missed when I had not been paying attention and was instead thinking about my excellent play with Miss Lois and me as the big star.

FOUR THINGS I DID NOT KNOW ABOUT PLASTIC

1 Polyester carpet is made from recycled plastic bottles. That means one day I could be standing on a carpet made from a bottle I had a drink from and no even know it.

DID YOU KNOW YOU ONCE DRANK FROM ME?

CARPET TALKING

2 You can make one grown-up person's fleece jacket out of just twenty-five recycled bottles. Of course, they

I DRANK OUT OF EVERY BOTTLE USED IN THIS JACKET.

have to do special stuff like grind the bottles up, but still it's pretty cool that you could one day wear your bottle.

3 Even though it's good that you can recycle plastic bottles and use them to make other stuff, it's still not great, because when you finish using the other stuff, you have to throw it away and it has to go in the garbage because it can't be recycled again.

I GUESS YOU ARE GOING TO THROW ME AWAY IN THE GARBAGE.

CARPET COMPLAINING

🕇 It takes about five hundred years for a plastic bottle to break down and disappear into the earth.

I'M STILL HERE! I'VE BEEN HERE FOR 300 YEARS NOW!

BOTTLE IN THE GROUND

I found out all these things from Mimi after she said, "Don't you feel bad?" when I was throwing my plastic water bottle into the recycling bin in the lunchroom. Mimi had learned it all when she had been paying attention in Miss Lois's class. Mimi said she was going to keep her bottle and use it for lunch again tomorrow. That way she wouldn't have to feel guilty about throwing it away. Of course my bottle was gone and it was too late, so I got to feel guilty about polluting the environment all by myself. It was not a good feeling!

After lunch, we learned some more things about recycling.

FOUR THINGS I DID NOT KNOW ABOUT PAPER

1 It takes 500,000 trees to make the paper for all the Sunday newspapers each week.

2 The average person in America uses seven trees a year in paper, wood, and other stuff made from trees.

3 If all newspapers were recycled, we would save about 250,000,000 trees a year.

4 Every ton of recycled paper saves seventeen trees.

Miss Lois was full of excitement and energy about being green. I did not feel that way. My empathy power was feeling sad for the earth, for the trees, and for the world!

REGULAR LEARNING

After telling us all about paper recycling, Miss Lois said it was time to talk about our regular schoolwork again. How could she do that? How could she not know that saving the earth was 100 percent more important than studying clouds, or fractions, or even cursive writing, which I like and is fun because it's kind of like drawing! Superheroes can't suddenly turn off their hero energy to learn about cumulus clouds. That's the difference between real superheroes and pretend ones, and the difference between Miss Lois and me.

MIMI AND ME

When school finally ended Mimi and I were feeling the exact same way. Tired of it! Me because I wanted to use my energy to think of a really great way to help save the earth, and Mimi because she didn't like cursive writing and fractions and could hardly wait to get home to see Gwen.

When she said that I couldn't believe that I had forgotten all about Gwen. My super-power is like that: once it starts working I can't even think about anything else at all, except if I have to go to the bathroom. I never forget about that. It must be the same for all superheroes, because none of them ever wear diapers, even though you never see them going into bathrooms. Astronauts are the only grown-up people who sometimes wear diapers, and it's easy to know why. There's no other way.

I'll NEVER TELL.

MIMI AND I BEING SEPARATE

Mimi wanted to walk home super fast. It was hard to talk about our recycling project because she was too looking forward to seeing Gwen to concentrate on anything else. When you are excited about something it can be frustrating if you are in that excited place all by yourself, especially if you are trying to have a conversation with someone else.

GWEN

Gwen was so amazingly happy that we were home. She was waiting outside at the end of Mimi's sidewalk. That way she could look all the way to the corner and see us as soon as we turned onto our street. She must have been at Mimi's house all day, because all her stuff was put away and it looked like she had lived in Mimi's room with Mimi forever.

Of course we had to stop talking about our project as soon as we saw Gwen. Sometimes it's hard to change over to something new when you are still really full of energy about the old thing. Because of this happening I was a little grumpy at Gwen for about a minute . . . but I got over it pretty fast.

Once we had all talked for a while, Mimi was a little more excited to be thinking about our superheroes of conservation project. Gwen said that she had done a recycling project about plastic bottles last year. I was pretty surprised that Miss Lois's great idea about doing projects to save the earth was also someone else's idea too. Gwen said everyone in third grade did projects about recycling and conservation. Sometimes she knows more about stuff than we do, but that is only because she is a year older than us. As soon as Gwen said "plastic bottles" Mimi said, "We have to do our project about plastic bottles too!"

WHY I COULD BE MAD

1 Mimi was totally being bossy about the project and not talking to me about it before so we could decide together like a team.

2 She was being with Gwen more than she was being with me.

WHY I WASN'T MAD

1 A plastic bottles project was perfect for us because we both felt guilty about just throwing them away.

2 It was nice of Mimi to make Gwen feel like she was important, because she was probably feeling all alone.

3 It was great to have Mimi feel full of energy about the project like I was.

WHAT IS EASY

Saying, "Let's do an amazing, totally important project about plastic bottles that will help save the earth!"

WHAT IS HARD

Figuring out what that amazingly totally important project about plastic bottles that will help save the earth will be.

WHAT YOU SHOULD DO IF YOU CAN'T THINK OF ANYTHING

A parent or a teacher would say, "Read a book." Mimi or I would say, "Time to watch

Unlikely Heroes," which is what we did right away. *Unlikely Heroes* is our most favorite show ever, and it was the perfect show to be watching when we were thinking about how we could be heroes ourselves. I couldn't believe it, but Gwen had never seen it before. Because of that Mimi and I decided that she needed to see the tape of our top five favorite episodes. That way Gwen would love it for sure.

TOP FIVE EPISODES OF UNLIKELY HEROES

1 Girl saves man from drowning by using her clothes as a rope. She helps pull him out of the water.

2 Pet pig saves his family from a burglar by trapping the burglar in a closet.

3 Man lifts car off of dog who was run over. Dog only has a broken leg.

4 Cat meows and wakes up family when there is a fire.

5 Baby calls 911 and he can't even walk yet.

I had to go home before the end because it was a school night and I'm never allowed to stay over at Mimi's house for dinner on a school night. Mom has lots of rules about stuff like that. It was super hard to leave because Mimi and Gwen were still watching *Unlikely Heroes* and my favorite part was about to be happening. I love it when the baby pulls the phone onto the floor and the noise scares the cat.

WHAT SHOULD NOT BE HAPPENING

Mom and Dad were being funny at dinner, and we were having artichokes, which is my most favorite vegetable ever, but still I was not 100 percent completely feeling normal. I could not stop thinking about Mimi and Gwen over at Mimi's house having lots of super-type fun without me. I was thinking about it so much, I almost forgot to do my one conservation thing for my chart.

I was just going to turn off the lights like before, but Mom was in her bedroom using the laptop computer and that was the only extra light that was on. She likes to take the computer in there when she is thinking about buying stuff online. That way Dad can't know about it and be grumpy about her spending money. It's always a good time to try to get her to buy me something new too, so I said, "What are you buying?"

"I'm throwing this ugly thing away and getting myself a new one," said Mom, and she pointed to her old gray fleecy jacket. "I can't decide between getting a new brown one or a black one." I was shocked. "Mom! You can't buy a new fleecy! You have to keep this one. If you throw it away, that's like throwing twenty-five plastic bottles right into the garbage can!" I didn't know if this next part was true, but I said it anyway. "Plus, that fleecy is probably going to take over five hundred years to disintegrate! It's going to be sitting in the earth forever!"

Of course Mom was pretty surprised. "Who told you that?"

"We learned it at school," I said. "And if you loved the earth then you would keep your old jacket and not buy a new one. It's important to be green!" Suddenly I was a superhero of conservation right in my own house, and it felt great!

Mom does not like to be told that she can't buy stuff. "Okay, Little Miss Green Pants, what if I donate it to charity so some-one else can wear it, or make a pillow out of it? Would that be okay? Can I buy a new jack-et then?" Sometimes you have to take what you can get, so I said, "I'd get the brown one—it's totally cuter," and then I did a

Green Pants victory dance all the way to my room. Now I had something to write about.

Saved one fleece jacket from the garbage.

I was so filled with good feelings that I decided to make a comic about it to show Mimi and Gwen, and now I was not feeling sad about them being together without me anymore.

SAVE THE EARTH

WHAT MADE ME NOT HAPPY AGAIN

Right before bed I looked out at Mimi's window. I was holding Chip-Up to show her how happy I was. She was standing there with Gwen and they were waving and laughing

SUPER SIZE

and passing Willoughby back and forth. They were having way more fun than a normal Willoughby night. If normal-size Willoughby was a regular happy night, then tonight he would have been super-jumbo-size!

I should have been super happy for them, but I couldn't do it. I kept trying to think good thoughts, but still the bad thoughts kept coming through.

GOOD THOUGHTS

1 Mimi is my best friend and she would never do anything to hurt me.

2 This exact same thing happened when Max moved in next door and it all turned out fine.

3 We can all be friends together.

BAD THOUGHTS

1 Maybe she is not hurting me on purpose but she is so busy having fun she's not even thinking about me at all.

2 Max is a boy and Gwen is a girl who is sleeping over at Mimi's house every night. It is completely different.

3 Why do they need me when they have each other and all their own special secrets?

The good-thoughts-bad-thoughts circle is not a good thing to have in your brain when you are trying to go to sleep.

RAINING

Sometimes when you are feeling sad it is nice for the weather to be rainy. That way the outsides of the world match up with what you are feeling on your insides. After breakfast I went over to Mimi's house to get her. Gwen didn't seem very happy when we left, so she was probably glad it was raining too. Mimi's mom had a table all set with pencils and paper supplies so Gwen could sit in the dining room and do her homework. Suddenly I felt pretty lucky that we were going to get to go to school.

MORE SAD

Learning about recycling today made me feel even more sad than yesterday. Every time I had to throw something in the garbage I just imagined it sitting buried underground forever.

GUM WRAPPER

At lunchtime we watched everyone throw plastic bottles into the recycling bin. Hardly anyone threw plastic bottles into the garbage anymore. That was good, but still it would have been better if they just took their bottles home to use again for the next day. Mimi said that that was what we should try to do as our project. Somehow make everyone use their same bottles over and over again. I tried to sound cheery and excited, but I was not 100 percent feeling very full of energy about anything today.

HOW TO MAKE A BAD DAY WORSE

Study the multiplication tables!

Marta said there was some kind of trick that let you use your fingers to cheat when you did the number nine multiplication tables but she couldn't remember exactly what it was. So that was not so helpful. Robert Walters said he was going to ask his cousin because his cousin knew all about cheating. This was not such a big sur-prise and not hard to imagine.

MY COUSIN WILL KNOW HOW TO DO THAT. HE IS A CHEAT EXPERT.

MY BAD DAY WAS NOT SO BAD AFTER ALL

Mimi could not wait to get home to see Gwen. I pretended I was excited about that too. I did not want Mimi to know I was feeling bad inside. It was the kind of thing I would have told Augustine Dupre about, except she was in France for three weeks, so I couldn't. Augustine Dupre is my grown-up friend who lives in the fancy apartment in my basement. She is a good listener and an excellent solver of problems, so it really was bad luck that she was not around right now. She spends a lot of time in France because she is a flight attendant.

Gwen was happy to see us again. Mimi's mom was there too. She said it had been a hard day. Then she gave Mimi some money so we could all go and buy ice cream. This was not a normal afterschool thing for her to do. While we were eating ice cream Mimi wanted to know all about Gwen's day. Mimi was probably imagining that she had missed out on a lot of fun stuff. This kind of imagining was not true.

WHAT GWEN DID THAT DAY

1 Homework while Mimi's mom vacuumed the house.

2 Reading while Mimi's mom talked on the phone.

3 Grocery shopping with Mimi's mom.

4 Sitting in a chair at the bank for a really long time with no magazine or anything to look at while Mimi's mom talked to the bank people.

5 More homework while Mimi's mom put the groceries away.

It was no surprise that she was overjoyed to see us. She had had a very horrible, boring day.

WHAT HAPPENED NEXT

1 I went home and had dinner.

2 Mimi called me to tell me that Gwen was going to get to come to school with us. And that even though she was a year older she was going to be in our same class. "That's great!" I said. Even though I was not 100 percent sure that it was.

At least my conservation chart was easy to fill out.

Will reuse my plastic water bottle every day.

After that I decided to make my bottle more beautiful by drawing on it and gluing on some jewels.

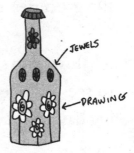

JEWELS

DRAWING

GOOD NIGHT

When I looked out my window Gwen was holding Willoughby and Mimi was holding Bunny. I held up Fluffy. It was that kind of night.

WALKING TO SCHOOL

It was weird walking to school with Gwen, and then when Sammy and Max showed up it was even more weird because suddenly we were a whole gang. Sammy knew he wasn't supposed to say anything about Gwen's parents being gone, so he started asking her all sorts of strange questions instead. She probably thought he was crazy, but I could tell that he was trying to be sneaky and find out if her parents were spies. He was asking her stuff like . . .

Do you practice kung fu or karate at home?
Is your house the kind with a secret room in the basement?
Do you have a big satellite dish on top of your roof?

Do you have lots of cool-looking remote controls all over?

When we finally got to school Gwen whispered, "What's wrong with him?" I couldn't answer her back because we were all going to the same class and Sammy would have for sure heard me. And then right before we went into the room Mimi said, "I have to tell you something." This sounded very mysterious and exciting, and it filled my head with questions and wondering, which is not a good thing if you are supposed to be concentrating on schoolwork instead.

ALL ABOUT GWEN

Pretty much the whole morning was all about Gwen. She got a desk near the back of the class, and when the rest of us were learning the stuff that she already knew, she just did her homework. Miss Lois said that she was going to let Gwen work with Mimi and me on our recycling project even though she had already done one last year at her regular school.

Miss Lois said, "There can never be too many cooks in the kitchen when it comes to saving the earth." That is a saying I know all about, because sometimes Mom says it when she is complaining about some of the parent meetings she goes to for school. What it really means is that everyone wants to be the boss and no one wants to be a helper. And usually if you have too many bosses then people get into fighting arguments about who gets to make the rules.

This is not something I was wanting for our plastic bottle project, and I was secretly hoping that Gwen was not going to turn out wanting to be top cook!

LUNCHTIME

Gwen, of course, had lunch with us. Mimi would not tell me what her big secret was, so I knew it had to be about Gwen. Now that she was with us all the time, it was going to be hard to find out what it was. We sat with two of the other Graces while we had lunch.

Gwen said she had met only one other Gwen in her whole life, so she thought it was pretty cool to have so many Graces around every day at school. I'm sure she wouldn't

have thought it was cool if she had to be called Just Gwen for the rest of her school life.

MIMI'S SECRET

Gwen was having a good time talking to Grace F., so Mimi was able to get us to go to the bathroom alone. As soon as the bathroom door shut, Mimi said, "Gwen thinks I gave her Willoughby to keep! She is sleeping with him, and last night I even heard her crying on him! What am I going to do?" When someone asks you something that you can't even imagine the answer to, you have to just say something like "Wow," or "Oh, no."

Willoughby is Mimi's favorite stuffed animal ever since she was born. When you love something that much, and have it for that long, you usually want to keep it for the rest of your life.

MIMI AND NORMAL-SIZE WILLOUGHBY

We could not stay in the bathroom forever, so finally we had to leave even though we did not have any brilliant ideas about how to solve Mimi's problem. It was not an easy problem to fix.

ANSWERS WE THOUGHT OF AND WHY THEY WON'T WORK

1 If Mimi just asks for Willoughby back, then Gwen will not have the stuffed animal she already loves, and she will cry even more and be sad that her parents are missing her birthday and she is stuck here with us.

2 If Mimi asks Gwen to pick a different stuffed animal to love, then Gwen will not have the stuffed animal she already loves, and she will cry even more and be sad that her parents are missing her birthday and she is stuck here with us.

3 If Mimi could find another Willoughby, she could give that one to Gwen and then she could get her own old Willoughby back. This seemed like the best idea, but Mimi has never in her entire life seen another Willoughby anywhere. Willoughbys are not like Graces.

4 Mimi could ask her mom to help, except that her mom already saw Gwen with Willoughby and said to Mimi, "That was very nice of you to let Gwen have Willoughby to help her feel better."

I didn't say anything about it but there was one thing that I was thinking about stuffed animals that was not going to help Mimi. All stuffed animals are not the same. Some you like, some you don't, and some you love. The weird thing is that you can't

make the love thing happen on purpose—some stuffed animals have love magic for you and some just don't.

MY FANCY BOTTLE

I was 100 percent glad that I had decorated my water bottle, because as soon as Mimi saw it she did a lot of forgetting about the whole Willoughby problem. I could just tell. Gwen said it was a fantastic idea and a great way for everyone to keep using bottles over and over again.

She had lots of craft ideas about how to decorate the bottles, and suddenly without even doing lots of thinking about it, we had our great idea for our passionate plan for saving the earth. If we were real superheroes, we would have been flying around the room in excitement!

This reminded me to tell Gwen that she should draw her costume for the superheroes of conservation project. That way she could be in the model we were going to make about all of us flying to save the poor red panda from extinction.

She said she was going to work on it after lunch when everyone else was studying the times tables for the one hundredth boring time. She already knew them all by heart. Even the really hard ones like the sevens, the nines, and twelves. She was lucky!

DOUBLE GREEN ME

When someone is jealous or wish they had what someone else already has, you can say they are green with envy. If someone is just happening to be doing a project about saving the earth, then you can say they are being green. And if both these things are going on at the exact same time, then you can say that person is double green.

I was double green about Gwen's super-great awesome superhero of conservation costume. It was fantastic! If we were all real superheroes, she would have for sure been the leader and Mimi and I would be the helpers and not one bit sad about that at all.

SPECIAL EARS SO YOU CAN HEAR REALLY WELL

MASK LIKE AN OWL

RADIO AROUND HER NECK TO HEAR A DISTRESS CALL

BELT THAT HAS ALL SORTS OF SUPER GADGETS

CAPE THAT HELPS YOU TO FLY

BOOTS WITH SPRINGS ON HER FEET SO SHE CAN BOUNCE

Gwen said her most favorite animals in the whole world were owls. This was an excellent pick for a superhero costume because owls can turn their heads all the way around to the back and look behind them. This would be a good extra if you are a superhero.

When Sammy saw Gwen's drawing he said, "I knew it! Your parents are spies! A regular person could never think of all those gadgets and stuff."

Then Robert Walters said, "Really? Cool! I wish my parents were spies. Is there a secret spy room in your house?" Miss Lois had to interrupt the class because suddenly everyone was getting all excited about Gwen being part of a secret spy family.

Miss Lois said, "Now, class, let's settle this right now." Then she asked Gwen the big important question. "Gwen, are your parents spies?"

Gwen smiled a funny smile and said, "No, Miss Lois, my parents are not spies."

"Fine," said Miss Lois. "Now we can finish our lesson."

Miss Lois thought we were all finished with the spy stuff, but she was wrong. She wasn't thinking about how a real spy daughter would never in a million years say that her parents were spies. A real spy daughter would lie about it every time.

I could tell that everyone in the class was thinking about the same thing I was, because even though Miss Lois was telling us all important information about how tomorrow was presentation day for our animal mascots, we were still all sneaking back looks at Gwen.

SAMMY'S NEW BEST FRIEND

Sammy was waiting for Gwen, Mimi, and me when it was time to walk home. Even though we were standing next to Gwen, he kept trying to get closer so he could walk next to her. The sidewalk is only big enough for three people to walk together in a line. If there is a number four person, that person has to walk in front of or behind the other three. By the time we got home I was the one walking behind.

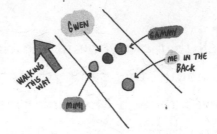

I was surprised about it but Gwen didn't seem to mind Sammy asking her all sorts of questions. It was like she was suddenly famous.

SAMMY'S PROJECT

Sammy told Gwen that he and Max were going to do some kind of special Tae Kwon Do can-chopping for their conservation project. He said they were going to show everybody that recycling cans could be fun and good for the earth at the same time. "Sounds great," said Gwen. And I couldn't tell if she was making fun of Sammy or if she really thought chopping cans was a cool idea. Suddenly she was seeming more mysterious, even though I didn't believe for a minute that she really was part of a spy family.

WHAT I DID THAT WAS UNUSUAL

Mom let me have dinner over at Mimi's house, and it was a school night. She said it was a special occasion since we were doing our recycling project together. That way we could work on it before and after dinner. Gwen was really helpful about looking up information on the red panda. It hardly took us any time at all to put our presentation together.

WHAT WE KNOW ABOUT THE RED PANDA

1 The red panda is super cute!

2 They are only a little bit bigger than a normal housecat.

3 They live in China, India, Laos, and Nepal, as well as a couple other places in Southeast Asia.

4 They sleep up in trees during the day and move around at night. This is called being nocturnal.

5 They eat mostly bamboo but sometimes they also eat berries, fruit, and roots.

6 Red pandas are endangered because their

homes are disappearing. People are cutting down their trees to use the wood and then

 building farms and towns where the trees used to be.

I'm starting to think that mostly 'when you think about saving the earth you are going to be sad. It is not a feel-good problem.

WHAT HAPPENED IN MIMI'S ROOM

As soon as we finished our project we went upstairs to Mimi's room. Mimi wanted to start working on the scene we were going to make out of clay. I'm not allowed to have clay in my room but Mimi's mom is really picky about her downstairs being clean so she likes Mimi to keep all that kind of stuff in her own room.

Gwen and I sat on the bed while Mimi looked for the clay. Her room is a huge mess, but she says she likes it that way. She always seems to find the exact thing she is looking for, even if you can't imagine how she could do it. While we were waiting I noticed that Gwen had picked up Willoughby. Mimi gave me a look that said, "See! She's got him!" and then she found the clay.

Mimi is much better at making characters than I am, so she made the red panda, the tree, and her own superhero. We couldn't make our clay superhero costumes as good as the ones we had drawn, but still, from far back they looked pretty good.

Gwen said it would be really cool if we could make a movie, like the kind people make with clay. Then our superheroes could swoop in and grab the red panda and fly off with him. Of course none of us could do that sort of thing, but still it gave us the idea to make our superheroes be flying, and that was better than having them just walk up to the panda. It is not so easy though to make superheroes look like they are flying.

After a while we called Mimi's dad and he helped us make that part of it. He's really good at construction stuff.

SAVING the RED PANDA
BY GRACE, MIMI AND GWEN

MIMI'S DAD'S BIG IDEA

To go downstairs and eat ice cream sand-wiches.

MIMI'S BIG IDEA

While we were eating our ice cream Mimi's dad asked Gwen what she wanted to do for her birthday. I had totally and completely for-gotten to remember that we were probably going to have a party for her. Gwen said she didn't know, and then that's when Mimi had her big idea. Mimi said, "I know a great idea! Let's go to one of those places where you can make your own stuffed animals."

And I knew exactly why she had sudden-ly had this big idea. It was a great way for her to get Willoughby back. Gwen would fall in love with a new fancy stuffed animal and then she wouldn't want Willoughby anymore. It was brilliant and perfect! But that was only until Gwen said, "Ewww. Those places are for babies. I already did that when I was five."

Mimi was not going to give up, though. "It could still be cool," said Mimi. "There's one at the mall that has all sorts of cool older stuff too."

"Now, Mimi," said Mimi's dad, "this is Gwen's special day, so she gets to decide. If you really want to go to  that place at the mall we can do that on your birthday."

"No," said Mimi. "I don't want to go there on my birthday."

"Well, good, then it's settled. Maybe you girls should work it out and let me know what you decide," said Mimi's dad, and then he left the room shaking his head.

IT'S NOT EASY TO FIX EVERYTHING

My empathy feelings were suddenly working super hard, and that was because both Mimi and Gwen were sad. Mimi because her excellent plan had not worked out, and Gwen probably because she was sure her birthday was going to be terrible. I was wishing with all my energy that I could think of a great way to solve both Mimi's and Gwen's problems at the same time. But I could tell that that was probably not going to happen.

There are lots of fun things you can do on your birthday, but most of them are not so fun if you are not with your best friends. Just when I was thinking that I wouldn't be able to think of anything, Mimi's dad came back into the room. He said, "Girls, this is just a suggestion. We could get a group together and go out to one of those Japanese restaurants. You know, the kind where they do the fire show at your table. I'll let you talk about it. Let me know." And then he was gone again.

I was surprised, but suddenly Mimi was all excited about the idea. She said the chefs twirled knives and even made volcanoes out of onions. It sounded pretty great. It took Gwen a minute to think about it, but then she said, "Yeah, that sounds like fun." One problem solved; now just one to go.

DINNER

Mimi's mom is a great cook, so it's always nice to eat over at her house. They eat stuff that I'm surprised I even like. Weird stuff like asparagus and clams and olives—grown-up food. The only thing they never have is sushi, and that's too bad for Mimi because she likes it almost as much as I do. I try to get Mom to order it when Mimi is over at our house—that way she gets to have some.

After dinner we all went up to Mimi's room to work on our plastic bottle project. Gwen said she thought it was important to scare everyone first with facts about what happens if you just throw away your plastic. That way people would want to recycle more. This was not a hard thing to do. Everything about pollution and garbage is 100 percent scary and sad.

FACTS ABOUT PLASTIC

1 Recycling plastic saves two times more energy than burning plastic in an incinerator.

2 Americans use 2,500,000 plastic bottles every hour, and most are just thrown away.

3 Recycling a single plastic bottle can conserve enough energy to light a light bulb for more than five hours.

4 The average American drinks about 167 bottles of water each year. That is about 50 billion plastic bottles a year for the whole country. Almost 38 billion of those are not recycled and are instead just thrown away.

5 It will take almost five hundred years for a plastic bottle to decompose in a landfill.

There were a lot more facts, but sometimes a little information is just perfect and maybe even better than too much information. It was all saying the same thing anyway, which was that if you didn't recycle your plastic bottle, you were hurting the earth, and that was really bad for everyone.

Finding out all this information was making us feel like we really had to help the earth.

SAVING THE EARTH

When I got home I still had to do my one conservation thing for my chart. I wanted it to be something big and important so that I would feel better about the world before going to bed.

I walked all over the house but I couldn't find anything big and important to do. I tried to get Mom not to flush the toilet after she used it, but she said that was disgusting. In the end I just brushed my teeth without letting the water run.

Brushed teeth without letting
water run in the tap.

It hardly seemed like any savings to the world at all. But that was how this whole recycling thing was working out anyway. It didn't really make much difference if only one person was doing all the recycling all by themselves. Everyone had to do it together or else it wouldn't work out.

I made Mom and Dad promise not to run the water while they brushed their teeth too. So in the end, that made me feel a little better.

TOOTHBRUSH

GOOD NIGHT TO MIMI AND GWEN

I flashed my lights and looked out my window to say good night to Mimi and Gwen, but they were not there. I was kind of glad about that. I did not want to see Gwen holding Willoughby and Mimi being all sad with Bunny. I let Chip-Up sleep on my bed with me. I was sad that he was not a real dog. Something soft and warm and furry would have been perfect for tonight. I was going to

have to remember to start bugging Mom and
Dad about a dog again.

LOOKING AROUND MY ROOM

When I woke up the next morning I just lay
in bed under the cozy covers and looked

around my room. Some-
times a big idea can hap-
pen when you are not
even expecting or think-
ing about it.

LOOKING SOME MORE

BIG IDEA

BREAKFAST

I asked Mom for some French toast for breakfast. French toast is something I like to eat when my empathy power is hard at work. It's my superhero breakfast. Mom said, "French toast? Well, you haven't had that in a while." She was 100 percent right. I have not been feeling my superpowers lately, even though I am supposed to be a superhero of conservation on top of my regular empathy power.

I was glad that tomorrow was Saturday, because that was perfect for my big plan of action.

PRESENTATIONS

Today was the first day of presentations. Mimi, Gwen, and I don't have to do ours until next week. This was perfect, because mostly all you have to do during pre-sentations is sit in your

chair and look like you are paying attention. So I had lots of time to think about my plan for tomorrow. I even had time to draw up a poster.

When it was lunchtime I could hardly wait to show my poster to Gwen and Mimi. I was surprised when Mimi said she wanted to be part of the sale too. She loves her stuff so much, she usually doesn't even let other people borrow her things. It was hard to imagine her letting anything go . . . even for money. Then, when Sammy found out Gwen was going to be there, he said he had some stuff he could sell too. We didn't see Max at lunch, but I was pretty sure he was going to want to be there as well. Pretty much everyone likes the chance to make money.

The good thing about having other people selling stuff was that it madethe sale bigger and more exciting—plus they could also help put up the posters. There was only one rule and that was. . . you can't sell junk!

MISS LOIS SAYS YES

At the end of the day I asked Miss Lois if having a yard sale counted as a thing for the conservation chart. She said that getting people to reuse products that already exist counted a

lot. She said she was
sorry that class was over
because she would have
told everyone about my
sale. Then she said that

she would be excited to hear all about it on
Monday morning when I came back to
school. Having Miss Lois be excited about
me and my project did one big thing. It made
me smile.

WHAT MOM SAID

After school I had to go home and ask Mom
for permission to go to the photocopy store.
She doesn't like for me to wander all over
town without knowing where I am. She's
lucky that a new photocopy store opened up
only three blocks away. That way she doesn't
have to do anything but say yes when I

ask her. Before that she had to drive me to the old one because it was too far away to walk. Mostly she doesn't ask what I want to copy, and if she doesn't want to know, then I don't tell her.

If I were a mom and saw five kids who were me, Mimi, Gwen, Sammy, and Max all waiting to get permission to go to the photocopy store, I would be suspicious. I would think, "What are those kids up to?" But not Mom. I think she just thinks, *Oh, good, they're leaving—now I can get some peace and quiet.*

ADVERTISING

You have to put up posters everywhere or else people won't know you are having a sale. Mostly the best places to put them up are at corners. That way the customers see them from all the directions. After the posters were up, we didn't hang around together at all. Getting stuff ready for a sale is hard work and you have to be organized, so we all went home to get ready.

WHAT IS NOT EASY TO DECIDE

There are some things that you just know are going to be easy to let go of and that is because they are not so special.

VASE

← NECKLACE

MIRROR WITH JEWELS

There are other things that are much harder than you thought, and that is mostly because they have a story with them.

JACK O' LANTERN PURSE THAT I GOT LAST YEAR FROM MRS. LUTHER

FAKE DIAMOND RING THAT DAD GAVE ME AS A JOKE

EXTRA NIGHT-LIGHTS THAT WERE PRESENTS

When I was all finished organizing, I had two whole boxes filled with stuff and my room was much neater and more organized. Mom could not be unhappy about that.

Secretly I was hoping to make twenty dollars—that way I could buy something fun and new to wear to Gwen's birthday party. Mom gives me money to buy presents for parties, but unless it's a special occasion I don't usually get to have presents for myself too. If I try to ask she just says, "You've got enough stuff already."

I was lucky about my conservation journal tonight. Mom forgot to turn the light out in the bathroom when she was finished.

Turned out light that was not needed since no one was in the bathroom.

SAVING THE EARTH ON A SATURDAY

I set my alarm for extra early—that way there would be enough time to get ready before everyone came to the sale. Most people like to go to sales early. That way they can find all the extra-good stuff before anyone else gets there. I was glad that Mimi and Gwen were waiting outside for me, because the big folding tables were way too big for me to set up all by myself. I guess Mom must have heard the garage door open because both she and Dad were suddenly standing in the driveway in their pajamas. Now Mom was curious and full of questions.

"Do you know what time it is?"

"What are you doing out here?"

"What's going on?"

"Mimi, does your mother know you are here?"

"What are all these boxes?"

Just then Sammy and Max showed up. Sammy said, "Good morning, Mr. and Mrs. Stewart. Are you helping with the sale? I've got some great stuff here. Maybe even something you'd like to buy?"

I think Sammy was kind of showing off

because Gwen was there. He's not usually that talky around parents.

"Grace, I need to see you in the kitchen," said Mom. While we were walking away, I heard Dad say, "I'll give you a hand setting up the tables," so that was good news.

Mom had lots to say. Mostly she was just saying the same thing over and over again but in different ways, and that was pretty much, "You can't have a yard sale without asking first. You can't have a yard sale without asking first." When I said, "But I thought you'd be happy about me cleaning my room and getting rid of stuff," she just held up her hand. That's Mom's way of saying I don't want to hear any more about it.

She started to make her coffee, so I just stood there watching her until finally she said, "Oh, go and help your friends. I'm up now."

VICTORY!

MOM'S COFFEE IN HER FAVORITE CUP ALWAYS PUTS HER IN A GOOD MOOD.

WHAT IS NOT SO EASY ABOUT A YARD SALE

Knowing how much to charge for your stuff is not easy. If the price is too high, then no one will buy it. If the price is too low, then you will lose money because you could have maybe charged a higher price and made even more money. It's all very tricky.

When I got back outside, Mimi and Gwen were already finished setting up Mimi's stuff. She was only selling five things. I couldn't believe that was it. I know for certain that Mimi has loads of stuff she doesn't use anymore. Mimi said it was hard to give things up. Every time she put something in the "to sell" box she thought, *What if I need that one day?* And then she'd take it out and keep it. She said it took all night just to find the five things on the table. Gwen was shaking her head while Mimi was talking. She said, "It was unbelievable."

SAMMY'S STUFF

As soon as I saw Sammy's things I said, "Sammy, you weren't supposed to sell junk. No one is going to buy all this."

"It's not junk!" said Sammy. "It's all good stuff. See this glass jar?" Sammy was holding up an old mayonnaise jar. It didn't have the label on it anymore, but I could tell it was a mayonnaise jar because Mom buys the same kind and I recognized the shape and the green lid. "It's an excellent jar for catching fireflies. Once I had twenty-five fireflies in this jar all at the same time. It's a lucky firefly jar."

I couldn't believe Sammy, so I said, "Well, no one is going to buy your lucky jar, because they don't even know it's a lucky jar. It just looks like an old mayonnaise jar that should be thrown into the recycling bin!"

"Then I'll make a sign or something," said Sammy. I could have stood there all day and argued with him about his junk, but I was more excited to set up all my good, amazing, and not-junk things on my table. Sammy would understand everything when my cash box was full of money and his was still empty.

SETTING UP THE YARD SALE

I set up all the big things in the back and all the small things in the front, and that way Gwen would not be able to miss the most important thing of all. That way Gwen would see it for sure. She was helping Mimi set up her five things on the little card table next to me.

MIMI'S TABLE

Mimi kept rearranging everything to make it look like more stuff, but five things look like only five things no matter how you set them up.

MY TABLE

I was pretty excited about my table. It was like the excellent sandwich filling in between Sammy's junk table and Mimi's tiny table. For sure customers were going to walk straight over to me and buy up all my stuff.

Just as soon as I had finished putting on the last price tag, Mom walked over with her coffee. She spent a lot more time looking at Sammy's table than I would have thought, but that was mostly because she was reading all the notes he was writing to put on his junk. Finally I just had to get her attention away by asking her what she thought of my table.

Instead of saying something like, "Oh, Grace, what a great table," or "What a wonderful and thoughtful display," Mom said, "I can't believe you are selling Wee Tiny Mee Mee! Don't you remember how you used to carry her around with you everywhere you went? We weren't even allowed to leave the house without her. She went everywhere with us.

"Do you remember that one time you left her at the pumpkin patch? You were so upset, just crying and crying. So we just had to drive all the way back to the pumpkin farm to get her. By the time we got there it was dark, but the farmer was very nice and gave us flashlights so we could look for her. Do you remember how excited you were when Daddy found Wee Tiny Mee Mee sitting up on a little pumpkin? It was a beautiful, warm, starry night. I'll never forget it."

"Wee Tiny Mee Mee?" said Sammy, and I could tell he was making fun of me. Mom has absolutely no clue how embarrassing she can be. I grabbed Wee Tiny Mee Mee from Mom and shoved her under my table. "Okay, I won't sell her. Happy?" Now I could tell that she knew I was feeling bad because she said, "I'm sorry, honey. Seeing Wee Tiny Mee Mee reminded me of that story. I haven't thought of that night in ages. It reminded me of when you were little. It's a sweet story."

I had to stop Mom before she 100 percent embarrassed me with gushiness, so I said, "It's okay, Mom. I'll keep Wee Tiny Mee Mee. Can we not talk about it anymore?"

I was glad when Gwen interrupted us by saying, "Oh my gosh, it's so cute!" And I knew right away, without even looking, that she was pointing at Owly.

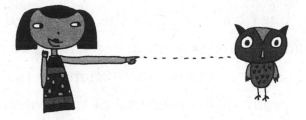

MY BIG PLAN

Gwen sees Owly.
Gwen buys Owly.
Gwen forgets about Willoughby.
Mimi gets Willoughby back.
Everybody is happy.

WHAT HAPPENED TO MY BIG PLAN

"How come you're selling this?" said Gwen. She was holding Owly, and I could see that Mimi was smiling. I hadn't told Mimi my big plan, but I could tell that she had figured it out and was 100 percent understanding it.

"I have too many stuffed animals," I said. Owly really wasn't even one of my favorites. I think Dad won him at a carnival or something. He wasn't that special to me, but I didn't say that because I wanted Gwen to think he was super special. "He's only two dollars," I said.

"I don't have any money," said Gwen. "I left all my money at my real house."

"Are you sure?" I asked. I couldn't believe my big plan was going to fail all because of two dollars.

"I'll buy it for you," said Mimi. "You could pay me back when you get home." I could tell she was desperate.

"No, it's okay," said Gwen. "I'm not really allowed to borrow money." Mimi looked like she was about to cry. It was a good thing that a bunch of strangers were walking up to us, because that made us concentrate on other things, at least for a few minutes.

MIMI TRYING NOT TO CRY

WHAT I COULD NOT BELIEVE

I could not believe that all the new people were looking at Sammy's table, and what was even more surprising was that they were buying his junk. In only a couple of minutes he sold four things, and I didn't even sell one single thing. His junk was selling faster than all of my good stuff. And it was all because of his notes. Everyone loved his notes.

FIREFLY JAR ←

COLLECTION OF NAILS IN A BOX ↓

MARBLE PYRAMID ↙

FLAT STONE COLLECTION ↙

LUCKY FIREFLY JAR. THIS JAR HAD 25 FIREFLIES IN IT.

I FOUND ALL THESE NAILS IN ONE MONTH JUST WALKING HOME FROM SCHOOL.

THESE MARBLES HAVE MAGNETS IN THEM SO YOU CAN MAKE COOL STUFF WITH THEM.

FLAT STONES ARE EXCELLENT FOR SKIPPING ALONG THE WATER!

THE FOUR THINGS SAMMY SOLD

WHAT HAPPENED NEXT

"Three dollars and fifty cents!" said Sammy, holding up his money.

"Well, your stuff is only selling because of your notes," said Mimi.

"Well, don't get mad at me," said Sammy. "It was Grace's idea. Why don't you just write your own notes?"

Sammy is not a boy who likes to pick a fight. Sammy is not even a boy who knows if you are trying to pick a fight with him.

Sammy is just Sammy. And Sammy's idea was a great one, even if he thought it was mine, which it wasn't.

EVERYTHING HAS A STORY

I had to run inside and get some paper so Mimi and I could write notes for our stuff too. We wanted to get finished before more people showed up and spent all their money at Sammy's table. But sometimes, if you really think about something and why you have it, and how you used it in your life, you can change your mind about giving it away.

VASE I WON AT A FAIR

PENCIL I USED IN SCHOOL WHEN I GOT 100% ON MY MATH TEST

TWO THINGS I TOOK OFF MY SALE TABLE

MIMI'S SALE TABLE

Writing notes was not a good idea for Mimi, because after writing about her stuff she decided she liked it so much that she couldn't sell any of it. She and Gwen went back to her house to take her stuff inside so it wouldn't get sold by accident.

While they were gone, I put Owly in a bag under my table. That way no one could buy him. I still wasn't ready to give up on helping Mimi. A good superhero always has more than one plan of action, and I just had to think of another one.

MAX

Max finally showed up while Mimi and Gwen were at Mimi's house. I told him he could use Mimi's table to sell his stuff. Max said he didn't have anything to sell because he had sold all his old stuff before he moved next door to Mimi. He said he was there to shop. He spent a lot of time at Sammy's table saying things like "I can't believe you are selling this. This is so awesome! I've got to get this." It was very annoying!

When he finally got to my table he only had fifty cents left to spend. I let him have a plastic box that was marked for one dollar. Sometimes you have to make deals if you want to make a sale. It was better than nothing.

I was hoping some girl customers would come by because they were probably not going to be thinking that Sammy's collection was so awesome and amazing. They were going to be looking for girl stuff.

WHAT WAS A BIT OF
A SURPRISE

Sometimes girls can be really hard shoppers.
I thought for sure that the girls who came by
would just snap up all my great stuff no problem, but that was not what happened. The
girls really liked to bargain. One girl even
tried to get me to sell two almost brand-new
Barbie dolls for only ten cents each. And it
wasn't even like she had only twenty cents.
Her purse was full of dollar bills—I saw
them. Sometimes you have to be tough or

else your entire table of really great stuff will get sold for almost nothing.

I finally said I would sell the dolls for fifty cents each. The girl seemed really happy because the original price was a dollar each, so she thought she was getting a real bargain. She probably thought she was a super shopper, but I was happy to get rid of them. I don't play with Barbies anymore anyway.

THE SALE

I was pretty sure that Gwen noticed that Owly was gone, but she didn't say anything about it and I didn't talk about it either. We decided to end the sale at lunchtime. There is only so much fun you can have standing around in your front yard. Everyone counted up the money and this is how it all ended up.

MIMI

No money.

No things reused by anyone else.

SAMMY

$22.25

More than twenty things reused by
someone else—lots of it to Max.

ME

$12.50

Seventeen things reused by someone else.

I was a little bit upset that Sammy had
made more money than me, but mostly that
was because the sale had been my idea in the
first place. Sometimes you have to stop yourself from getting angry about something like
that, because the best thing is that everyone

is happy. Surprisingly even Mimi was happy, and she didn't make even one single penny.

Mom said we should donate all the rest of the stuff on our tables to charity. She said if we boxed it up in the garage, she'd take it over to the donation box the next time she went out. Sammy said he was just going to take his leftovers home, so Gwen and Mimi helped me pack my stuff up and put it next to the car.

WHAT WAS THE BIGGEST SURPRISE OF THE DAY

When Sammy was leaving with his box Gwen went over and asked him if he wanted to come out to dinner with us on her birthday. I couldn't believe it. Sammy looked like he couldn't believe it either, but he smiled.

He looked even happier when Gwen said it was the kind of restaurant where the chef does tricks with fire. Sammy is the kind of boy who would be excited about things exploding.

Gwen invited Max too, but mostly I think that was because he was standing right next to Sammy.

This was going to be the first time I had ever eaten with Sammy in a restaurant. Once he had pancakes at my house, but that had been a mistake invitation.

Sammy is the kind of boy who gets food stuck in his teeth and dribbles on his shirt. He was going to be a mess. Especially since this was the kind of restaurant where you use chopsticks instead of a fork. I was definitely not going to sit next to him.

Gwen seemed happy and kind of excited about her birthday when she got back from talking to Sammy and Max. She was not thinking the same things about Sammy that I was, and that was because she had never sat near Sammy while he was eating. She was going to be in for a surprise too!

WHAT WAS NOT THE BIGGEST SURPRISE OF THE DAY

When we went upstairs to Mimi's room Gwen started playing with Willoughby right away.

I could tell that Mimi was pretty upset that the Owly plan had not worked out. Poor Mimi. It's not easy to watch someone take over one of your most favorite things in the world. It's even harder not to say anything about it while you're watching it happen. Mimi was being great.

THE BOTTLE PROJECT

While we were in Mimi's room we finished up organizing the bottle project. We told Gwen that we had to come up with examples of how to decorate the bottles—that way even some of the really uncreative people in our class would be able to do it. There are some people who don't have brains full of ideas. You have to help these kinds of people out.

FOUR BOTTLE-DECORATING IDEAS

After we finished putting our posters together with the examples of how to decorate the bottles, and all the facts about recycling plastic, it was time for me to go home for dinner. Mom doesn't like it if I eat too many dinners at Mimi's house. She says she doesn't want me to be a burden to Mimi's mom, but I just think it's mostly because she misses me.

OUR NIGHTTIME

At dinner Mom apologized for telling the Wee Tiny Mee Mee story in front of my friends. I said, "Wee Tiny Mee Mee's name is almost more embarrassing than the story," and then we all laughed. I was only two years old when I named her Mee Mee. I called her that because I thought she looked like me. Dad added the Wee Tiny part because he thought it was funny. And then the nickname just stuck. It's kind of like me now with my crazy name of Just Grace—only I'm not laughing about that one.

I DID NOT EVER LOOK LIKE WEE TINY MEE MEE

NOT ACTUAL SIZE

ME WHEN I WAS TWO   **WEE TINY MEE MEE**

Mom was happy that I did not sell Wee Tiny Mee Mee. She said she was going to put her in my box in the attic. This is the place where Mom puts all my stuff that she says I'm going to one day want when I get older. I'm not sure she's right about that, but since I don't have to have the box in my room I'm okay with it.

After dinner I went up to my room to draw a comic card for Gwen. I also wanted to wrap up Owly to give to her on her birthday. If it was a birthday present she couldn't give it back. Plus I could tell that she really liked him. I was hoping she would be liking him enough to give up Willoughby.

WHAT I DID NOT DO BEFORE BED

I did not flash my lights to say good night to Gwen and Mimi. I did not want the last thing in my brain to be a picture of Mimi holding Bunny.

ALL BY MYSELF

Mimi and Gwen are gone for the whole day. Mimi's mom and dad took them to a big craft show that is two hours away. Gwen was excited about it because Mimi's mom said she was going to let her pick out a birthday present there. Her birthday is only two days away, so I guess she is getting kind of worked up about it.

Gwen's parents already sent her a present, but she is not allowed to open it until her birthday. It's a real skinny package so it must be jewelry or something. We were all trying to guess what was inside but Gwen made us stop because she didn't want us to guess right and ruin the surprise.

GWEN'S PRESENT FROM HER PARENTS

WHAT MAKES A DAY SEEM REALLY LONG

Spending the whole day with your mom while she does normal mom stuff. Now I could totally see why Gwen wanted to come to school with us.

The only fun thing we did all day was go to the store to buy Gwen a real birthday present. Mom said Owly didn't count as a 100 percent real present because he was a used item and he didn't cost anything.

I didn't argue with her even though she was totally wrong, because I could tell she was feeling sorry that I was lonely. A mom in a feeling-sorry mood is the kind of mom that just might buy her daughter a present even if it is not her birthday.

Usually Mom gets frustrated when we go present shopping. She says I take too long to decide on something. Today I was lucky that she was looking for some special beads to make herself some earrings. That way she wasn't rushing me.

← SUPER-CUTE PURSE WITH COLORED DOTS ON IT

POCKET THAT OPENS UP AND THERE IS A MIRROR INSIDE

GWEN'S PRESENT

Mom said that she liked the present I picked out for Gwen so much that she thought I should have one too.

MINE HAS FUN STRIPES.

MY PRESENT

Mom said it wasn't fair for both Gwen and me to have one and not give one to Mimi.

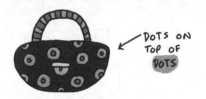

DOTS ON TOP OF DOTS

MIMI'S PRESENT

Then on the way home from the store Mom stopped at a bakery and we bought cupcakes.

WHO IS THIS MOM?

It was like a shopping alien had taken over her body or something. Mom was not acting normal at all.

MY REAL MOM WITH THE ALIEN

THE ALIEN MOM WITH ME

WHAT I SAW RIGHT BEFORE BED

When I flashed my lights and looked out the window I saw Mimi and Gwen both holding Willoughby at the same time. Each of them was holding one of his arms. They were of course really happy, for which I was 100 percent glad, but still I was wondering how it was going to work out in the end. Who was going to let go when it was bedtime?

WHAT IS SO GREAT ABOUT TODAY FOR GWEN

Tomorrow is Gwen's birthday. When you know you are having a birthday tomorrow you automatically have a great day today,

because you can't help but be filled with excitement, even if your parents are not there.

WHAT IS SO GREAT ABOUT TODAY FOR MIMI

Mimi had a great day yesterday and some of that feeling is still left over with her today. She said that last night in the middle of the night when she got up to go to the bathroom, she saw that Willoughby was on the floor beside Gwen's bed. She said that she thought that this was a good sign and that

maybe Gwen was getting ready to give him back. When someone is feeling good about something it is not a good idea to say that you think their reasons for being happy are not good ones. That is why I didn't say that maybe Gwen just dropped him by accident.

WHAT IS SO GREAT ABOUT TODAY FOR ME

Tomorrow is going to be a great day and I can't help smiling when I think about it. Gwen is going to love Owly and give Willoughby back to Mimi.

I was feeling so happy that when Miss Lois asked for volunteers to go first to present their con-  servation projects, I put my hand up. Tomorrow is going to be our day for that.

WHAT CAN MAKE A DAY SEEM TO LAST FOREVER

Thinking about tomorrow and still being stuck in today.

WHAT HAPPENED THAT WAS INTERESTING

Gwen asked Grace F. if she wanted to come out with us for the birthday dinner. Grace F. was really upset that she couldn't do it. She was already going to have dinner at her aunt's house for her cousin's birthday. She said that flaming volcanoes sounded a lot more exciting and fun than macaroni and cheese, which is what she was going to be eating.

WHAT ELSE HAPPENED THAT WAS INTERESTING

Nothing.

Miss Lois tried to get us all excited about our projects some more, but I was already completely full with excitement about tomorrow, so I stopped listening to her.

MY DRAWING

WALKING HOME FROM SCHOOL

Somehow Mimi and Gwen and I got to walk home all by ourselves. Sammy was not around, for which I was glad. Too much Sammy was not something I was completely used to or happy about. We talked about our recycling project a little bit, but mostly we talked about Gwen's birthday.

When we got to Mimi's house we all went and looked at the present from Gwen's parents again. Gwen said we could hold it if we promised not to shake it too hard or

guess out loud at what we thought was inside. She was 100 percent wanting to be surprised and 100 percent not wanting us to ruin it with our guesses.

DINNER

I could tell what we were going to have for dinner the minute I walked into the house. Mom has this silly way of asking Dad to order sushi for dinner. He always does the ordering because Mom says he does a better job with saying all the food names in Japanese.

When Mom wants sushi she plays her special sushi song on the CD player. I don't really know what it's called but the main part of the song says, "I'm turning Japanese oh yes I'm turning Japanese I really think so." It's kind of like their secret code. Mom plays the song, Dad hears it and orders the food, the doorbell rings, and then we eat dinner. I for sure couldn't tell Sammy about it or he would start thinking my parents were spies too!

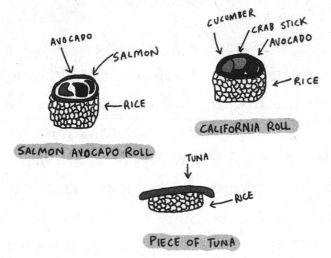

AVOCADO
SALMON
RICE
SALMON AVOCADO ROLL

CUCUMBER
CRAB STICK
AVOCADO
RICE
CALIFORNIA ROLL

TUNA
RICE
PIECE OF TUNA

WHAT I FORGOT

After dinner I went to my room, and as soon as I walked in I knew that I had completely forgotten to do my conservation chart yesterday. Now I had to find two things to do, which was going to be impossible because I usually even have trouble with the one thing.

I went downstairs. I was hoping that Mom and Dad were in the basement so I could turn off the lights in the kitchen and the living room, but they weren't. Dad was reading a paper and Mom was in the kitchen cleaning up the sushi stuff.

Mom was about to throw away the stuff from dinner, but I stopped her just in time. Sometimes great ideas just happen in a second, without even any warning. That's my favorite kind!

Saved paper bag from the garbage by using it as wrapping paper. Used plastic decorations from sushi dinner to decorate package. That's two things to make up for forgetting yesterday.

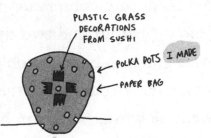

PLASTIC GRASS
DECORATIONS
FROM SUSHI

POLKA DOTS I MADE

PAPER BAG

GOOD NIGHT, NOBODY

Mimi and Gwen were not at Mimi's window, but Chip-Up and I waved anyway, just in case.

TODAY IS THE DAY

Mom said I couldn't have French toast for breakfast because there wasn't any bread left, because I had been eating so much

French toast lately. That was kind of disappointing, but not a big enough sadness to even hurt the day.

Mimi's dad drove us to school with all our stuff for our plastic bottle presentation. It's a good thing that Miss Lois said we could do it in the art room—that way we could use all their cool supplies and we didn't have to bring in even more stuff. Mimi's dad kind of wanted to stay and watch, but Miss Lois has a rule about parents being in the classroom. The rule is No Parents in the Classroom, so he just had to go to work like normal.

OUR PRESENTATION

It took a while for all the regular morning school stuff to be finished, but finally we were all allowed to line up and go to the art room. Miss Lois had let Gwen, Mimi, and me go earlier, so everything was set up and perfect. All the kids wanted to know why they were taking their lunch boxes with them. Ten o'clock in the morning is not the time to eat lunch, so it was kind of confusing.

Miss Lois was a big help getting everyone organized. Teachers go to school for that kind of thing, so she knew exactly how to say the right thing in the right order to have it all work out. When we went to the front of the room to do our presentation, everyone was sitting in a chair looking forward with a water bottle on the desk in front of them. Only Robert Walters was looking down, and that was because he was trying to sneak-eat some raisins. Miss Lois caught him though. She has eagle eyes for catching eating in the classroom when you are not supposed to.

I was a little bit nervous, so Mimi said she would go first. Mimi and I took turns telling everyone the facts about plastic bottles, and then Gwen told them about the art project of decorating their water bottles so they would be excited to reuse them every day. All they would have to do is rinse them out every night.

At the end of the talking, Mimi lifted the cover off the display we had made. Miss Lois had to tell everyone to please calm down and sit down because they all thought it was so excellent and were getting out of their seats to see it better.

The only bad part of the project that we didn't think about was the using-glue part. Glue takes a long time to dry. We all had to leave the decorated water bottles in the art room and couldn't have them back until tomorrow, when they were 100 percent dry.

There was lots of whining and complaining, but Miss Lois said it would be helpful to the earth if we could just all use the water fountains for one day. I thought that she would maybe be mad at us about it, but she said, "Team one has done an excellent job. Who wants to go next?"

Sammy and Max volunteered, and that was probably because Sammy wanted to be sure to do his project before Gwen had to leave and go back to her old school. Plus, they had been collecting a lot of cans in Max's garage, and Max's mom said she was getting tired of tripping over cans every time she wanted to use the car. Max said he was worried that she would throw them out if they didn't use them soon.

SUPERHERO

FLOWER GARDEN

SQUARES

HAPPY FACES   CAMOUFLAGE

SOME EXCELLENT BOTTLES
THAT WERE MADE

The whole rest of the day was a blur. That is what Mom says when her day goes by really fast and she can't think of any special one thing that stood out.

BIRTHDAY DINNER

I was ready to go to dinner way before it was time to leave. Mom said I had to wait at home until it was time to go. She let me watch an episode of *Unlikely Heroes* because she said she was tired of me pacing the floor.

How could I not be excited? It's pretty hard to be still when your brain is thinking of flaming volcanoes, twirling knives, great presents, and making your best friend's problem disappear.

WHAT WAS SURPRISING

When I was finally allowed to go to Mimi's house, Sammy was already there, and he had on a shirt with buttons. I had never seen Sammy in a shirt that wasn't a T-shirt before. It almost made him not look like Sammy anymore.

I was glad that Mimi's parents were almost ready to go. I was way too excited to be just sitting around and waiting some more. Gwen said that she was going to open all her presents when we got back from dinner. Mimi's mom has a rule about presents being opened after you eat the birthday cake.

Both Gwen and Mimi were wearing new clothes that they got at the art fair. Mimi noticed my new purse and loved it, so I had to give her hers.

Of course Gwen noticed Mimi's right away. I could tell that she was wishing she had one too, so when Mimi's mom wasn't looking, I gave her hers.

Gwen went to the bathroom to open it

so Mimi's mom wouldn't see. Of course Mimi's mom noticed it as soon as she came out of the bathroom. Girls always notice fashion stuff, even grown-up lady girls. I forgot about that part.

Sammy went to get Max, and then finally we left.

WHAT WAS GREAT ABOUT THE RESTAURANT

EVERYTHING!

SOME COOL TRICKS

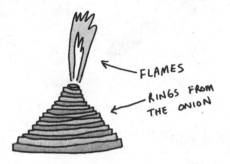

Making a flaming volcano out of an onion.

Cutting up shrimp in the air and then throwing it right into your mouth.

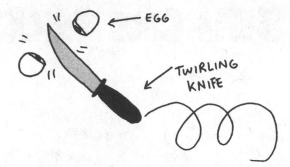

Twirling a knife in the air and having it cut a hard-boiled egg.

WHAT ELSE IS FUN

Super-great fancy drinks in cool cups that you get to keep.

It was pretty much the most fun I had ever had at a restaurant. I didn't even really mind when Sammy's shrimp came flying over the table and landed in my water glass. Those chopsticks can be tricky . . . plus it made everyone laugh.

At the end of the dinner all the restaurant people came over and sang a special Japanese happy birthday song for Gwen. Then they took our picture and put it in a card so she could keep it.

I am definitely going back there for my birthday.

BIRTHDAY PRESENTS

Mimi's mom made Gwen a purple cake, which was great because that's Gwen's favorite color, so of course she loved it. I was hoping that Gwen was going to open the present from her parents first because I really was dying to see what was inside. Gwen said she wanted to save it for the end, because it was the most special one. Plus, her parents were going to call at eight so that they could listen while she opened it. Knowing that made me want to see inside even more!

Suddenly I was feeling nervous about her opening my second present. I was glad that she was opening other stuff first.

Max gave her a journal and a fancy pen. Sammy gave her a cool wood and glass box that came with all sorts of craft supplies so that you could decorate it yourself. It had a little secret drawer in the back which you could only open with a special code. It was hard to imagine Sammy picking out such a great present, but he said he had done it all by himself.

GLASS TOP

PLACE TO DIAL SECRET CODE

SECRET DOOR

Finally it was time to open my present. "Another present from you?" asked Gwen. She was saying that because I had already given her the purse. Gwen is a careful opener, so it took her a few seconds to get the paper off.

"It's Owly!" said Mimi.

"I thought you sold it!" said Gwen. I could tell that she was happy to have it because she was smiling and she gave it a hug.

Just then the phone rang. Gwen ran to get it and was so excited that she almost tripped over all her birthday stuff that was on the floor. Mimi's mom put the phone on speakerphone so we all heard Gwen talking to her mom and dad.

It took her about two seconds to rip their birthday package open. She was not a careful opener anymore. All that was inside was a birthday card with a picture of a puppy on the front. Gwen opened the card and screamed! There was something exciting inside but none of us could figure out what it was. Mimi's mom took the phone off speakerphone so Gwen could talk to her parents in the kitchen. She was still doing lots of screaming and saying "Oh, thank you, thank you, thank you!" Finally she came back and we could tell that she had been happy crying.

She held the birthday card out for us to see and said, "Look! Look! Isn't he cute?" "Very cute," said Mimi's mom. "What are you going to name him?"

And then we all understood. Mimi screamed, "You got a puppy? A real puppy!" Now everyone was excited! I couldn't believe it! I didn't even know Gwen wanted a puppy. A puppy was the best birthday present ever. I wanted one. Mimi wanted one. Max probably wanted one. Everyone loves puppies.

"I get to pick him up next week," said Gwen. For the whole rest of the night we could not stop talking about the puppy. We all wished he were there at that very minute.

Well, probably all of us except for one, because Sammy doesn't like dogs.

WHAT IS HARD

It is hard when a perfect fun day has to end and you know that the next day coming up is probably not going to be as perfect or as fun. That night when I flashed my lights with Chip-Up, I was happy to see Gwen holding Owly and Mimi holding Willoughby. I let Chip-Up sleep with me, and all over again I was a little double green.

CHIP-UP
COVERED UP TOO.

But it was different this time because I was smiling. And I didn't know it, because my superpower is not one that lets me see through walls, but right next door Gwen was smiling.

OWLY NOTE

OWLY IS THE BEST STUFFED ANIMAL FRIEND EVER. HE IS FILLED WITH ♥

OWLY

POPPY PICTURE

And Mimi was too.

THE END

WHAT GRACE WILL BE THINKING ABOUT IN HER NEXT BOOK

055948385